HELLO, SNOW!

Hope Vestergaard   Pictures by Nadine Bernard Westcott

Melanie Kroupa Books

Farrar, Straus and Giroux · New York

For my father,
a fearless sledder
—H.V.

For Julie M.
—N.B.W.

Text copyright © 2004 by Hope Vestergaard
Illustrations copyright © 2004 by Nadine Bernard Westcott
All rights reserved
Distributed in Canada by Douglas & McIntyre Ltd.
Color separations by Prime Digital Media
Printed and bound in the United States of America by Phoenix Color Corporation
Designed by Nancy Goldenberg
First edition, 2004
10 9 8 7 6 5 4 3 2 1

NOV 2 4 2004

www.fsgkidsbooks.com

Library of Congress Cataloging-in-Publication Data
Vestergaard, Hope.
    Hello, snow! / by Hope Vestergaard ; pictures by Nadine Bernard Westcott.— 1st ed.
        p.   cm.
    Summary: A young child bundles up and discovers the delights of a snowy day.
    ISBN 0-374-32949-4
    [1. Snow—Fiction.   2. Father and child—Fiction.   3. Stories in rhyme.]   I. Westcott, Nadine Bernard, ill.   II. Title.

PZ8.3.V71266He 2004
[E]—dc21
                                                                          2003045509

Hello, morning . . .
Goodbye, night.
I see something
Cold and white!

Hello, Daddy.
Goodbye, bed.
Let's get ready,
Sleepyhead!

Hello, pants.

Goodbye, knees.

I don't want
You guys to freeze!

Hello, sock.
Goodbye, toe.
Hold on, piggies—
In you go!

Hello, sweatshirt . . .
Goodbye, me!

Hello, snowsuit.
Goodbye, tum.
Zip it up and . . .
OW!
My thumb!

Hello, hat.
Goodbye, ear.
HEY!
It's pretty dark in here!

Goodbye, Mommy . . .
Here we go!

Through the door
And . . .

Hello, sunshine!
Hello, wind!
Snowflakes tickle
On my chin.

Goodbye, snowplow.
Hello, heap!
WOW!
This mountain's pretty steep!

Hello, snowball.
Pack it hard.
Roll it round
And round the yard.

Hello, neighbor!

Hello, pup . . .
Hey, what's that
You're digging up?

Hello, sled.
Let's climb the hill—

Goodbye, Daddyyyyyyyyy!

CRASH!

We spill!

Brush the snow off.
Hello, friend.

Goodbye, tears . . .
Let's go again!

Goodbye, puppy!
Goodbye, flakes!
Hello, snowman—

HIT THE BRAKES!

Hello, Mommy.
Time to go?
You made cocoa?

GOODBYE, SNOW!